FIG 59372085527516

WITHDRAWN

Silly Sue

Sign Language for Actions

by Dawn Babb Prochovnic
illustrated by Stephanie Bauer

Content Consultant:
William Vicars, EdD, Director of Lifeprint Institute
and Associate Professor, ASL & Deaf Studies
California State University, Sacramento

magic
wagon

visit us at www.abdopublishing.com

For Angela, my sister and friend, who actually prefers cats—DP
For Annabel…the fourth Bauer girl—SB

Printed in the United States.

♻ PRINTED ON RECYCLED PAPER

Written by Dawn Babb Prochovnic
Illustrations by Stephanie Bauer
Edited by Stephanie Hedlund and Rochelle Baltzer
Cover and Interior layout and design by Neil Klinepier

Story Time with Signs & Rhymes provides an introduction to ASL vocabulary through stories that are written and structured in English. ASL is a separate language with its own structure. Just as there are personal and regional variations in spoken and written languages, there are similar variations in sign language.

Library of Congress Cataloging-in-Publication Data
Prochovnic, Dawn Babb.
  Silly Sue : sign language for actions / by Dawn Babb Prochovnic ; illustrated by Stephanie Bauer ; content consultant, William Vicars.
      p. cm. -- (Story time with signs & rhymes)
  Includes "alphabet handshapes;" American Sign Language glossary, fun facts, and activities; further reading and web sites.
  ISBN 978-1-60270-672-9
  [1. Stories in rhyme. 2. Dogs--Fiction. 3. English language--Verb. 4. American Sign Language. 5. Vocabulary.] I. Bauer, Stephanie, ill. II. Title.
  PZ8.3.P93654Sil 2009
  [E]--dc22
                                                                    2009002404

Alphabet Handshapes

American Sign Language (ASL) is a visual language that uses handshapes, movements, and facial expressions. Sometimes people spell English words by making the handshape for each letter in the word they want to sign. This is called fingerspelling. The pictures below show the handshapes for each letter in the manual alphabet.

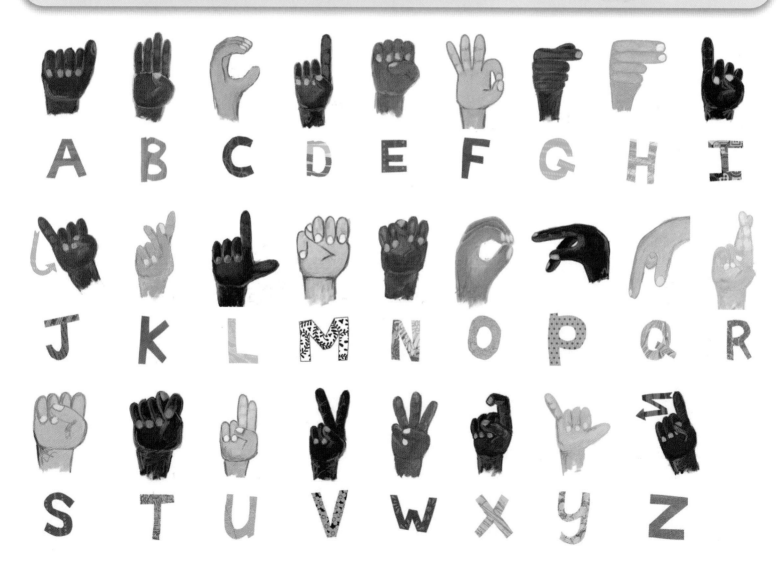

My dog's name is Silly Sue.
We've been friends since I was two.
We can **play** the whole day through.
And when we **play** she's silly, that Silly Sue.

play

Wake, wake, wake, Silly Sue.
I can't wait to play with you.
Wake, wake, wake, Silly Sue.
Wake, Silly Sue, it's morning.

6

wake

Silly Sue wakes up and runs outside.
Once out back, she finds the slide.
Then she takes a belly ride!
And when she **slides** she's silly, that Silly Sue.

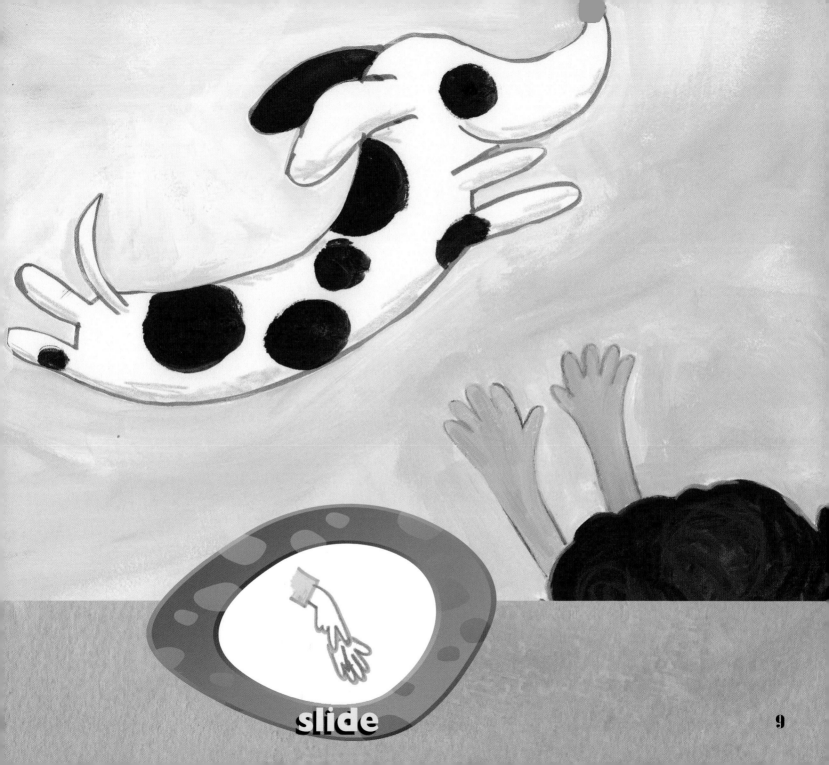

slide

Slide, slide, slide, Silly Sue.
I'll go down the slide with you.
Slide, slide, slide, Silly Sue.
Slide, Silly Sue, I'm ready.

slide

Silly Sue can whirl and twirl and **spin**.
She twirls, then falls, then twirls again.
She's on her feet, then on her chin.
And when she **spins** she's silly, that Silly Sue.

12

spin

Spin, spin, spin, Silly Sue.
I feel dizzy, how 'bout you?
Spin, spin, spin, Silly Sue.
Spin, Silly Sue, we're dancing.

spin

Silly Sue **runs** fast when we play chase.
She's the one who sets the pace.
I have yet to win a race.
And when she **runs** she's silly, that Silly Sue.

run

Run, run, run, Silly Sue.
You chase me, then I'll chase you.
Run, run, run, Silly Sue.
Run, Silly Sue, I'll follow.

run

Now we're hungry, time to **eat**.
Sue will sit down by my feet.
I'll give her a doggy treat.
And when she **eats** she's silly, that Silly Sue.

eat

Eat, eat, eat, Silly Sue.
One for me and two for you.
Eat, eat, eat, Silly Sue.
Eat, Silly Sue, it's yummy.

eat

After eating, Sue will **sleep**.
Snuggled down into a heap.
She snores loud, and she snores deep.
I'll bet her dreams are silly, that Silly Sue.

sleep

Sleep, sleep, sleep, Silly Sue.
Here's a bedtime kiss for you.
Sleep, sleep, sleep, Silly Sue.
Sleep, Silly Sue, **I love you**.

I love you

American Sign Language Glossary

eat: Tap the fingers of your flattened "O Hand" to your lips. It should look like you are putting food into your mouth.

I love you: Hold your hand in front of you with your palm facing out and your thumb, pointer finger and pinky finger all pointing up. It will look like you are combining the handshapes for the letters "I" "L" and "Y" into one sign.

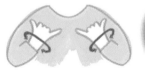

play: Hold your "Y Hands" in front of you and quickly twist your hands from side to side in a playful manner. It should look like your hands are dancing playfully.

run: Hold your "L Hands" in front of you with your palms facing down and the tips of your thumbs touching. Now bend and straighten your pointer fingers as you move your hands forward. It should look like you are showing your legs moving when you run.

sleep: Put the palm of your hand in front of your face then gently slide your hand down to your chin and touch your fingers to your thumb. While you are moving your hand, close your eyes and bow your head. It should look like your hand is shutting your eyelids and bringing your head into a resting position.

slide: Put your left hand in front of you with your palm facing up, and put the fingertips of your right, upside-down "V Hand" on the palm of your left hand. Now quickly slide your right fingertips off the palm of your left hand, ending with the fingertips of your right "V Hand" pointing forward. It should look like a person going down a slide.

spin: Hold both hands in front of you with one pointer finger pointing up and one pointer finger pointing down. Now twirl the tips of your pointer fingers around each other in opposite directions. It should look like you are showing the motion of something spinning.

wake: *Use the sign for "wake up"* by holding both hands near the outer corners of your eyes with your palms facing each other and your pointer fingers touching your thumbs. Now quickly move your pointer fingers up and your thumbs down and open your eyes really wide. It should look like you are showing your eyelids popping open when you wake up.

Fun Facts about ASL

Proper names such as "Sue" are often fingerspelled. A special tradition in the Deaf Community is to give individuals a name sign. This is a special sign that is created by someone in the Deaf Community. It can be used in place of fingerspelling to identify an individual by name. It is generally considered disrespectful for people in the Hearing Community to create name signs for themselves or others.

Most sign language dictionaries describe how a sign looks for a right-handed signer. If you are left-handed, you would modify the instructions so the signs feel more comfortable to you. For example, to sign "slide," a left-handed signer would hold the palm of the right hand in front of the body and use the left upside-down "V Hand" to make the sliding motion.

Some signs use the handshape for the letter the word ends with to make the sign. For example, the word play ends with the letter "Y" and it is signed with the "Y Hand." It is easier to remember how to make the sign if you remember how to spell the word!

6 7 8 9 10

Signing Activities

Simon Says in Sign: This is a fun game for a classroom or a group of friends to play together. Gather the players in an area that will allow for plenty of movement, and select someone to be the first signer. For each round of play, the signer begins by saying, "Simon says _____" and signing an action word, such as run. When players hear this command they should run in place until the signer gives another "Simon Says" command. Occasionally the signer should sign a new action word without saying "Simon Says." A player is out and must sit down if they perform any actions without the signer saying, "Simon Says_____." Play continues until only one player remains standing. That player becomes the next signer.

Freeze: This is a fun activity for a classroom or a group of friends to enjoy together. Gather in an area where you can play some music and where there is plenty of space to move around. Turn on the music and select someone to be the signer. The signer begins by making the sign for an action word, such as spin. Participants should do the signed action to the rhythm of the music. When the signer shouts "freeze," all participants must hold their bodies completely still. They can't move until the signer makes a sign for a new action word, then the fun continues. Take turns being the signer until everyone playing has had a turn.

Additional Resources

Further Reading

Costello, Elaine, PhD. *Random House Webster's Concise American Sign Language Dictionary*. Bantam, 2002.

Heller, Lora. *Sign Language for Kids*. Sterling, 2004.

Sign2Me. *Pick Me Up! Fun Songs for Learning Signs (A CD and Activity Guide)*. Northlight Communications, 2003.

Warner, Penny. *Signing Fun*. Gallaudet University Press, 2006.

Web Sites

To learn more about ASL, visit ABDO Group online at **www.abdopublishing.com**. Web sites about ASL are featured on our Book Links page. These links are routinely monitored and updated to provide the most current information available.